OUTside INside Poems

by Arnold Adoff
Illustrated by John Steptoe

Lothrop, Lee & Shepard Books
New York

Library of Congress Cataloging in Publication Data. Adoff, Arnold. OUTside/INside Poems. Summary: Poems reflect a child's thoughts inside and outside, describing what he sees and feels. 1. Children's poetry, American. [1. American Poetry] I. Title. PS3551.D6609   811′.5′4 79-22168 ISBN 0-688-41942-9 ISBN 0-688-51942-3 lib. bdg.

for
jaime levi adoff
and
the boys and girls
of
the yellow
springs perry
league
and
the little league
pirates

OUTside

the rain is falling fast   like the falling curtain
at the end of a school play
and the night sky is full of night winds
that
bend the branches down
on the old tree by
my bedroom window

OUTside

the branches scrape the shutters of the window
and
the leaves brush against the glass panes
in the swishing rhythms
of the n i g h t rains

INside

      the house is my room   and inside the room is my bed
      and
inside
      the bed is
          me   under the covers
listening to the
   outside tree

INside

      my room the light from the lamp
          that is shaped like
               that famous
               duck
                  shines
        on my pillow

        and i smile

INside

      the light is shining through my eyes   into my hollow head
      and
           along a tunnel of purple paper
      to
      my brain

INside

      my brain   the light of the lamp meets the noise of the bending tree
                                  and the falling rain
           and light
             covers
             noise
               with a blanket of yellow
                       clouds   and buttered pop
                                    corn
                                  lumps
   stuck together with brown sugar and morning dew

INside

       the longest second   and the shortest hour
       is
inside
       me
          and i am new

OUTside

on the school yard field
i am standing in my baseball shoes
and yellow hat

that
new glove
is hanging
from my hand
and
i am just too
small for
every thing i
need to be a star

INside

      the baseball glove   is my hand
      and
inside
      the fingers of my hand
                      are strands of golden wires
      sliding through
           my wrist bones   and up my arms
           to a secret
              central
              signal
              system
full of
flashing
      lights and creaking wheels and spinning dials

      all controlled by a green octopus
                eating
                  a
      peanut
      butter and tuna sandwich on toast
                while
                boasting
                  about
      his great
        games at first base
           at second
              base
           at third and
             home

OUTside

        are the black shoes

               with the black laces

               that never stay tied

       and the scrapes

       on their sides

           from every slow

              slide

out

   side of every bag

 and into

     every tag

INside

       my shoes are green socks   and inside each sock
                            is a tan foot
                   and at the end of
                     each tan foot
are five unhappy toes

INside

each toe is a bright red ribbon   leading through the ankle bones
and beyond the bending knees to
a central
    secret
    signal
    system

full of
flashing
 lights and spinning dials and whizzing wheels

 all controlled by identical
 centipedes
 eating
peanut
butter and pickle sandwiches on toast
 while
boasting about
 team work team work team work team work team
 work

OUTside

i am standing at home plate   watching that fast ball
leave the pitcher$_s$
hand
and travel in a straight
line into the   catcher$_s$
mitt
while the umpire
yells
strike three

three

out

INside

and starting just behind my eyes
                                    the longest rubber bands
                                        s t r e t c h   out
and travel through my head
            and down my neck
                                to meet the plastic ropes
                            that run up from my arms
        to a secret
            central
            signal
            system

full of
flashing
            lights and creaking wheels and spinning dials

        all controlled by a family of detroit tigers
                                        eating
        peanut
        butter and chopped liver sandwiches on toast
                                            while
                                            boasting
                                            about
            pouncing on the pitch
        or pouncing on the pitch
                                er

OUTside

       the ketchup and relish are dripping on my shirt
       in the middle
             of a hamburger
       in the middle of the team
                picnic

INside

    the thinnest silver circles
                slide down my throat
  and float across the river
        near my liver to a signal
              system
                   so
              central
                 and
              secret
  where a grandfather rhino
          is writing on the wall

  N
   eaTnEss iS All
        BUT IF u D
             rip don't
          S
           lip up
              on the
                ball

OUTside

      my pants are torn
      and there is a
           scrape
      on my knee

INside

      an eagle takes off
      from its nest
      and flies
         free

OUTside

the things that grow each day   keep growing into night
like my toe
            nails and head
                        hair   and fingers
and this
        best new
            set of teeth
                        that bite my good night snack
                                    to disappearing

INside

        are the ribbons and wires   and the thinnest silver chain
        that slide and wind and connect

                        the fingers to the   brain
inside
        the story of a smile
             while
                base
              ball players sleep

INside

the falling rain   and the bending tree
the longest second
and the shortest
hour
is
inside
me
and i am new